D1470351

Welcome to ALADDIN QUIX!

If you are looking for fast, fun-to-read stories with colorful characters, lots of kid-friendly humor, easy-to-follow action, entertaining story lines, and lively illustrations, then **ALADDIN QUIX** is for you!

But wait, there's more!

If you're also looking for stories with tables of contents; word lists; about-the-book questions; 64, 80, or 96 pages; short chapters; short paragraphs; and large fonts, then **ALADDIN QUIX** is *definitely* for you!

ALADDIN QUIX: The next step between ready to reads and longer, more challenging chapter books, for readers five to eight years old.

GOES FOR GOLD

**Read more ALADDIN QUIX books
featuring Geeger!**

GEEGER THE ROBOT GOES FOR GOLD

BY
Jarrett Lerner

ILLUSTRATED
BY
Serge Seidlitz

ALADDIN QUIX

New York   London   Toronto   Sydney   New Delhi

ALADDIN QUIX
Simon & Schuster Children's Publishing Division
1230 Avenue of the Americas, New York, New York 10020
First Aladdin QUIX hardcover edition April 2023
Text copyright © 2023 by Jarrett Lerner
Illustrations copyright © 2023 by Serge Seidlitz
Also available in an Aladdin QUIX paperback edition.
All rights reserved, including the right of reproduction in whole or in part in any form.
ALADDIN and the related marks and colophon are
trademarks of Simon & Schuster, Inc.
For information about special discounts for bulk purchases, please contact
Simon & Schuster Special Sales at 1-866-506-1949 or business@simonandschuster.com.
The Simon & Schuster Speakers Bureau can bring authors to your live event. For
more information or to book an event contact the Simon & Schuster Speakers Bureau
at 1-866-248-3049 or visit our website at www.simonspeakers.com.
Book designed by Karin Paprocki
The illustrations for this book were rendered digitally.
The text of this book was set in Archer Medium.
Manufactured in the United States of America 0323 LAK
2 4 6 8 10 9 7 5 3 1
Library of Congress Control Number 2022943256
ISBN 978-1-6659-1090-3 (hc)
ISBN 978-1-6659-1089-7 (pbk)
ISBN 978-1-6659-1091-0 (ebook)

For all my creator friends

Cast of Characters

Geeger: A very, very hungry robot

DIGEST-O-TRON 5000: A machine that turns the food Geeger eats into electricity

Tillie: A student at Geeger's school, and Geeger's best friend

Coach Keller: Geeger's gym teacher

Mr. Katz: Geeger's art teacher

Roxy, Gabe, Sidney, Arjun, Olivia, Mac: Other kids in Geeger's class, and also Geeger's friends

Ms. Bork: Geeger's classroom teacher

Chef Mike: The chef at Geeger's school

Contents

1

Field Day!

Geeger is a robot. A very, very hungry robot.

Geeger was put together by a bunch of scientists, then sent to a town called Amblerville. What does Geeger do in Amblerville?

He EATS!

Geeger eats all the food that the rest of the people of Amblerville don't want.

Expired beans. Moldy pasta. Mushy, gushy, super-slimy veggies. Those are just a *few* of the items Geeger chows down on.

Every night, after eating old yogurt and stale cereal and expired vegetables and rotten fruit, Geeger plugs himself into his **DIGEST-O-TRON 5000**. The machine sucks up all the food in the robot's stomach and— *Bzzt! Bzzt! BzZzZzZzZzZt!*— turns it into electricity. And that electricity helps power Amblerville's lamps, TVs, microwaves, video game systems, and dishwashers.

But Geeger does more than just **EAT EAT EAT EAT EAT** in Amblerville.

He also goes to school.

Geeger has learned LOTS since he started going to Amblerville Elementary School. For instance, he knows how important it is to have a good breakfast before a long day of learning and playing with his pals. And today it is *especially* important that Geeger has a good breakfast. Because today is Amblerville Elementary School's Field Day!

At first, Geeger was confused about what a Field Day could be. Was it a day for celebrating

fields? They *were* nice, the robot supposed . . . So green and big and open. Or was Field Day a day for celebrating someone named Field?

Maybe, Geeger thought, *this Field person was the first to put peanut butter on a banana*. THAT certainly deserved celebrating. Peanut butter and banana is one of Geeger's favorite food **combinations**—and he loves it even more if the peanut butter is **expired** and the bananas are mushy and brown.

YUM!

Fortunately for Geeger, he wasn't confused about Field Day for long. His best friend, **Tillie**, quickly explained it to him.

Field Day is a special day of school when all the students and teachers at Amblerville Elementary School gather outside and **participate** in a variety of athletic events. There are races and jumps, Hula-Hooping and hopscotching. There are even SNACKS!

Geeger couldn't be more excited.

There's one thing, though, that Geeger is MOST excited about. . . .

The *medals.*

There are three of them—gold for first place, silver for second, and bronze for third—and they are awarded to the winners of the last event of the day, a footrace across the entire length of the school's field.

And perhaps most exciting of all: Geeger really, truly believes that HE can win the footrace. He's pretty sure he's faster than every other kid at Amblerville Elementary School. He thinks he can outrun them all— even the fifth-graders who are taller than him!—and take home the gold medal.

Just thinking about winning that

big, shiny **disk** fills Geeger up with a buzzy energy. It feels like that one time his DIGEST-O-TRON mal-functioned and, instead of pumping electricity out into Amblerville, the machine sent it roaring back into *him*. Geeger wants to rush out the door and race to school right this minute.

But he knows he can't do that.

Not yet.

First, he needs BREAKFAST.

2

Lumps and Bumps

Geeger eats breakfast at record speed. If there were medals given out for the Fastest Eater of Putrid Fruit, Rancid Vegetables, Ancient Cereal, and Stinking Yogurt, Geeger would certainly take home the gold.

As the bot fills his mouth with

- an **assortment** of mealy apples
- bunches of limp, slimy celery
- boxes of cereal that lost their flavor ages ago
- tubs of yogurt that had once been silky white
  but are now a brownish green

he thinks about the field. The one behind Amblerville Elementary School. The one where, later today, the footrace will take place.

The field stretches from the edge of the playground to a distant row of pine trees. For the past week, Geeger has spent his recess time closely studying the field. He has **memorized** each and every one of its little lumps and bigger bumps. He knows where the first graders **stash** all the sticks and rocks they use when pretending to be pirates searching for hidden treasure. The bot has learned every single thing he needs to know about the field to help him get from one end of it to the other as fast as he possibly can— faster, hopefully, than anybody else.

Geeger eats. . . .

And eats . . .

And eats.

And as the bot packs his belly with

- green oranges and brown bananas

- soft, soggy mushrooms

- rock-hard granola

· eight different kinds of canned beans, all of which expired years before he was even built

Geeger closes his eyes. He imagines that afternoon's race. And he can see himself flying across the field, leaving all the other runners behind. He can see himself soaring over the finish line. He can see **Coach Keller** rushing over to him with the gold medal in her hands. He can see himself taking it from her and holding it high above his head so that it sparkles in the sunlight. Geeger can even hear his friends, **chanting** his name in their pride and excitement.

Geeger!

Geeger!

Geeger!

"Geeger?"

"Geeger?!"

"GEEGER!"

All of a sudden, Geeger snaps out of it.

"HELLO? GEEGER? ARE YOU IN THERE?"

Geeger knows that voice.

He grins, then shuts the door to his stomach, grabs his backpack, and hurries to the front door.

3

The Greatest Idea

Geeger pulls open his front door and sees none other than his best friend in the whole entire galaxy—and, in Geeger's opinion, the best human being in the whole entire galaxy.

"TILL-*eee*?" Geeger asks. He's extremely pleased to see her. But he's also a bit confused. Usually, Geeger meets Tillie at school. "WHAT are you *dooo*-ing here?"

Tillie pops up onto her toes, then sinks back down and gives Geeger her biggest grin.

"I was too excited about Field Day," she explains. "I couldn't wait any longer, so I left my house. But it was way too early to go to school, and so I was just going to go back. But then I had this idea. I thought I'd come here and pick you up and we could go to Field Day together!"

"THAT," Geeger says, **"is the GREAT-est I-dea in the HIS-tor-eee of I-deas."**

Tillie closes her eyes. And somehow, her grin gets even *bigger*.

"I thought so too," she says.

Then, opening her eyes back up, she adds, "So, are you ready, or what?"

Geeger tightens the straps on his backpack, closes the door behind him, and says, "I am READ-i-er than . . . than . . . than . . . than a REAL-*leee* READ-y RO-bot."

Tillie giggles, then leads the way over to the sidewalk and toward school.

For a block or two, the friends are quiet. Geeger admires the cloudless sky. He observes the breeze, gently moving the leaves in the trees. He lifts one of his metal fingers and notes the way the sun glints off the tip. Seeing it, Geeger can't help but think once more about the gold medal. . . .

"Ooh," Tillie says, breaking the silence. "I wonder if they'll have crafts again this year. Last Field Day, **Mr. Katz** set up a whole table of them. We got to make these super cool bracelets. And the snacks.

Geeger—wait till you see the snacks! And I'm so glad about **Roxy**. She gets to do the long jump this year, since last time she had a sprained ankle. She can *really* jump. And **Gabe**! I think Gabe is going to try to beat his Hula-Hooping record. Last year he kept going for three hours straight! It. Was. **AMAZING.** And the kickball game! The kickball game is SO FUN. It's always the best part of the day. Definitely my favorite. **You've GOT to play!**"

Geeger hears his friend. But he's

only kind of listening. Because he's still thinking about the gold medal, and the footrace, and all those lumps and bumps and **bundles** of sticks and piles of rocks he needs to make sure to avoid if he wants to win it.

"Do you THINK I am *gooo*-ing to WIN?" he asks suddenly.

Tillie's mouth is hanging open, like she had been in the middle of saying something. She closes it, then frowns up at Geeger.

"Win?" she asks. "Win what?"

"The RACE," Geeger explains.

"The ONE at *theee* end OF the DAY. I think I HAVE a *chaaance* to GET a gold MED-al."

"Oh," Tillie says. "Well, I—"

"I have been PRAC-ti-CING a LOT. And I am VER-*eee* GOOD at running right when the whistle blows. And I have MEM-or-IZED all *theee* lumps and BUMPS on the FIELD. And—and—*aaaand*—and I REAL-*leee* think I HAVE a *chaaance* to GET a gold MED-al."

Tillie doesn't say a thing. She just stares up at Geeger. Then, finally, she says, "Well, Geeger, I think—"

But that's as far as she gets.

Because all of a sudden someone is shouting:

"GEEGER! TILLIE! OVER HERE!"

Geeger turns his head, and sees two more of his classmates. **Sidney** is wearing a brand new pair of sneakers. Gabe has on a green sweatshirt with white stripes down the sides, plus a pair of matching sweatpants. The kids both lift their arms over their heads and say,

"FIELD DAY!
"FIELD DAY!
"FIELD DAY!"

Geeger and Tillie give each other

a grin, then join in on the chant.

"FIELD DAY!

"FIELD DAY!

"FIELD DAY!"

They keep it going for as long as they can. But then Tillie laughs, which gets Geeger laughing too. And Sidney and Gabe aren't far behind.

"Get ready, Geeger," Gabe says once he has recovered. "Today is FIELD DAY—also known as the best day of the whole entire school year."

Geeger grins down at his long metal feet, the tips of which sparkle in the sunlight.

4

PWEEEEEEEET!

When Geeger and his friends get to school, they find all of Amblerville Elementary's teachers gathered outside the front doors. It's a very strange sight. But a *thrilling* one too.

Ms. Bork steps out from the

crowd, wearing a skirt with a pattern of birds and frogs on it. She's holding a clipboard in one hand and a pencil in the other.

"Over here, friends!" she calls to Geeger and the others.

Ms. Bork says each of her students' names out loud as she checks them off on her attendance sheet, which is what she has clamped to her **clipboard**. Then, with a great big smile and a dramatic swoop of her arm, she says, "You may now proceed to Field Day."

Gabe leads the way around the side of the school and to the field behind it.

And as soon as they get a glimpse of it, Sidney gasps.

Tillie says, **"Whoa."**

And Geeger would probably both gasp AND say *whoa*, but the sight of the field has left him speechless.

The wide **expanse** of grass has been completely **transformed**.

Yesterday, it was a plain old field. A *nice* field, and one that Geeger had come to love dearly. But still— it was just a field. Now, however, it's covered in cones and ropes and poles and ribbons. There are streamers and flags and banners and tents. And there are kids—kids everywhere—running and jumping and laughing and shouting. The sight of it all makes Geeger's wires buzz. It makes his circuits sizzle. It makes him want to RUN RUN RUN RUN RUN.

But Gabe beats Geeger to it.

"My lucky Hula-Hoop!"

he cries, then darts off to the part of the field that has been set aside for Hula-Hooping.

Geeger, Sidney, and Tillie watch their friend go.

Then Sidney says, "There's Coach Keller! I think she's about to—"

PWEEEEEEEEET!

Sidney is interrupted by the shriek of a whistle.

Two seconds later, Coach Keller hops up on a chair and cries,

"WELCOME, WELCOME, WELCOME TO AMBLERVILLE ELEMENTARY SCHOOL'S ANNUAL FIELD DAY!"

All the students cheer. The teachers, who by now have made

their way to the field, cheer as well.

Coach Keller waits for the cheers to quiet down, then reviews the day ahead. She lists all the activities that kids can take part in, pointing to the area of the field where each one will take place. She makes sure everyone knows where the crafts table is located, where water and snacks will be passed out, and where to get a Band-Aid should anyone need one. Then she goes over the main events of the day: the juggling contest, the kickball game, the hopping **competition**.

"And last, but certainly not least . . . " Coach Keller concludes. "The big one! The main event! Drum-roll please!"

A bunch of teachers and almost all the students crouch down and drum their hands on their thighs. The *pat-pat-pat*-ing gets louder and louder and then, just when Geeger thinks it couldn't possibly do so, it gets even louder still.

PATTA-PATTA-TAPPA-TAPPA-PAT!

PATTA-PATTA-TAPPA-TAPPA-PAT!

At which point Coach Keller throws her arms up into the air and cries, **"THE FOOTRACE!"**

The crowd goes wild. And hearing all those kids, watching them cheer and shout, Geeger's thoughts leap forward. He's thinking about the end of the day again, to the moments just after the footrace. The robot imagines himself standing right where Coach Keller is, at the center of everything, raising a shiny gold medal high above his head while a crowd of kids cheer and shout for *him*.

"Now, don't forget," Coach Keller says while Geeger continues to **daydream**, "the three most important things about Field Day. Have fun. Do your best. And practice good sportsmanship by celebrating the achievements of others as well as your own. And with that—"

PWEEEEEEEEET!

"EEP!" Geeger yelps, the shriek of the whistle bringing him crashing back to reality.

And then Coach Keller hollers:

"LET THE GAMES BEGIN!"

5

The Games Begin

Geeger and Tillie start their day in the jump rope area. They each grab a rope—Tillie chooses a bright blue one; Geeger takes one that's yellow and pink—then get to it.

Tillie shows off some of her fanciest moves, then **attempts** a couple she's never done before. Geeger, meanwhile, takes it easy. He doesn't want to tire himself out. He needs to save as much energy as he can for the footrace at the end of the day. He also doesn't want to risk hurting himself. Imagine if he tried some difficult jump rope trick, only to fall over and dent his toe or knock his leg out of place? It would ruin his whole day!

After the jump ropes, Geeger and Tillie head for the snack table. The friends each take a bag of animal crackers and a juice box, then make their way to the crafts table. There they find all kinds of art supplies laid out on the table. There's also a stack of papers. Each one has instructions for a different project kids can do with the stuff on the table.

Tillie uses a small paper bag, some pipe cleaners, and a bunch of googly eyes to make a monster puppet.

Geeger, meanwhile, picks out a square sheet of bright green paper. With a little help from his art teacher, Mr. Katz, the robot folds it into a **hummingbird**.

"HEL-*looo*," Geeger says, holding his bird out to Tillie's monster.

"AH!" Tillie says, making her monster's paper bag mouth open wide as if in terror. "A talking bird!

A talking bird! **Someone HELP ME!**"

Geeger giggles, then says, "Do NOT worr-*eee*, Mis-TER mon-STER. I am a NICE bird-*eee*."

"Oh," Tillie makes her monster say. "Good!"

Geeger flies his hummingbird right up to where the monster's ear would be, if Tillie had given the creature ears. He wiggles it from side and side and says, "ARE *yooou* EX-cit-ed for *theee* FOOT-race? I REAL-*leee* hope Gee-ger WINS."

Tillie's monster puppet sinks down to her side. And in the blink of an eye, her silly mood is gone. All of a sudden her face looks serious. Even worried.

"Geeger . . . ," she says. "Remember that stuff Coach Keller said? The three most important things about—"

PWEEEEEEEEET!

"KICKBALL!" Coach Keller yells from the other side of the field. "WHO WANTS TO PLAY KICK-BALL?!"

Tillie's eyes pop open. Her whole face lights up. It's clear she has totally forgotten she was just in the middle of a sentence.

"Geeger," she says. "Let's go! It's already the best part of the day!"

She takes off, quickly joining a group of other kids who want in on the kickball game too.

But Geeger stays behind and watches Tillie disappear into the crowd. It's not because he doesn't want to play kickball. He does, especially because he knows it's Tillie's favorite part of the whole day. But Geeger *can't* play kickball. Not now. He'll tire himself out. He'll waste all his energy and have none left for the footrace. If he plays kickball now, there's no way he'll win the race.

Geeger turns himself around so he's not **tempted** to join the kickball game anyway. And as he's spinning, a distant sparkle grabs his attention. His eyes slide back toward it— and then focus on a faraway table. It's the only one that he and Tillie haven't visited yet. And Geeger has a guess about what must be on that table, shining the sunlight.

Geeger starts toward the table, and before he even reaches it, he knows he's right. He can see them lying there, glinting and gleaming.

The medals.

They're even bigger than he imagined. And each one has been stamped with a drawing of the front of Amblerville Elementary School, plus the word WINNER.

Geeger gazes at the medals for several minutes. And then—he can't help himself—he reaches out for the gold one. He's just about to pick it up when someone yanks on his arm.

Spinning around, he finds **Arjun** and **Olivia**.

"Geeger! Geeger!" Arjun cries. "We've been looking all over for you! You almost missed lunch. And you've got to come see. You're not going to believe it!"

"*Beee*-lieve WHAT?" Geeger asks.

But in his excitement, Arjun has already run off.

Geeger turns to Olivia for an explanation.

She grins and says, "Wait till you see what **Chef Mike** made you for lunch!" Then she hurries off too.

Geeger takes one last look at the medals. Then he shouts, **"Wait UP!"** and runs after his friends.

A Special Lunch

Geeger can smell lunch before he even reaches the tables where Chef Mike has set it up. The scent fills the robot's head with a familiar command:

EAT! EAT! EAT! EAT! EAT!

"Geeger!" says Chef Mike as soon as he sees him. "Right this way!"

Chef Mike waves Geeger down to the far end of the table, where he shows him a special silver tray. *Special* because it has a piece of paper taped to it, and on the piece of paper, Chef Mike has written, FOR GEEGER. And in the tray is a gloopy, gloppy, stinking, delicious-looking— for Geeger, at least—mess.

"It's all of last week's leftovers," Chef Mike explains, "blended together with a gallon of expired

FOR
GEEGER

milk and topped with a sprinkling
of some moldy cheese."

The next thing Geeger knows,
Chef Mike is plopping a bunch of
the stuff on a plate and shoving it
into the robot's hands.

"Enjoy," Chef Mike says with a giant smile.

Geeger stares down at the food. But his brain doesn't do what it normally does. It doesn't tell him to **EAT! EAT! EAT! EAT! EAT!**

"Geeger?" asks Chef Mike. "Is everything okay?"

Geeger makes himself nod. Then he says, *"Ummm...Ahhh...Errr...* YES. Ev-er-*eee*-THING is O-*kaaay.*"

Before Chef Mike can ask him anything else, Geeger grabs a fork and goes to join his friends. Most of them have already finished their meals. Now they're just talking, reliving their favorite moments from the day.

Geeger hears them—but doesn't really listen. He gazes at his plate of greenish-brown, lumpy, bumpy food and can't help but think about the field and the footrace. Any minute, the robot knows, Coach Keller will blow her whistle and tell all the kids who want to run the race to gather at the starting line. And it's like Geeger is already there, imagining every bit of it. His brain says, GET READY! GET READY! GET READY! It says, RUN! RUN! RUN! RUN! RUN! It says, WIN! WIN! WIN! WIN! WIN.

And then:

PWEEEEEEEEET!

"RUNNERS!" Coach Keller bellows. "THE FOOTRACE WILL TAKE PLACE IN FIVE MINUTES!"

Geeger finds a trash can and tosses his untouched lunch into it.

Then he takes a deep breath.

Because here it is ...

The moment Geeger has been waiting for.

The Footrace

Dozens of kids rush over to Coach Keller.

Geeger takes it nice and slow, wanting to **preserve** all the energy he can.

By the time he reaches the starting line, the bot is *buzzing*. He's full of more feelings than he can possibly count. There's excitement—and also nervousness. There's joy—and also **doubt**. And all of it—that whole big mess of emotions swirling inside of Geeger—makes his circuits shake and his wires quiver.

He tries to calm himself down. To focus. He reminds himself of all he needs to remember.

Take off right when the whistle blows.

Avoid the lumps and bumps.

Don't trip on the first graders'
stash of sticks and rocks.

Geeger feels a tap on his shoulder.

"Good luck!" someone says.

"You *tooo*," Geeger mutters, not
even bothering to look over.

"*Geeger*," the someone says again.
"It's ME."

Geeger finally turns to look.

And he sees Tillie.

"OH," he says.

The smile on Tillie's face melts away.

"Geeger," she says. "Are you okay?"

Geeger opens his mouth to answer. But before he can get a word out, Coach Keller shouts, "RUNNERS! ARE YOU READY?!"

Geeger refocuses.

Take off.

Avoid.

Don't trip.

"ON YOUR MARKS!" cries Coach Keller.

Geeger plants one foot behind the other. He bends his knees.

Take off.

Avoid.

"GET SET!"

Don't—

PWEEEEEEEEET!

Geeger **springs** off his back foot. And then he's *flying*, the air whizzing by him, roaring in his ears.

At first, there are kids all around him.

But within just a couple of seconds, things are a lot less crowded. Geeger is pulling ahead.

He can see a handful of the tallest fifth graders out in front of him. But with every stride, they're closer. A few more, and Geeger knows he'll be right up beside them.

LUMP! his brain shouts.

Geeger dodges to one side.

BUMP!

Geeger veers toward the other.

BIG LUMP!

Geeger dodges.

REALLY BIG—

This time, when Geeger moves to the side, he feels something crash into his hip.

But there's no time to look and see what it was.

Here comes some of the first graders' sticks and rocks!

JUMP! JUMP! JUMP! JUMP!
JUMP!

Geeger leaps, clears the pile of
pirate treasure, and lands. And when
he does, he sees an amazing sight.
There's no one else in front of him—
and no one else around him, either.
Geeger is in the lead! And the finish
line is just up ahead.

Just a little farther . . .

Just a few more strides . . .

And . . .

HE DID IT!

Geeger blows over the finish line. He throws his arms up over his head, slows to a stop, and turns around.

But Geeger doesn't see a crowd of proud, happy kids chanting his name. He sees a not-so-amazing sight. He sees his best friend in the galaxy, Tillie, down on the ground, grabbing at her knee, looking like she's hurt.

Geeger remembers how, one of those times he'd dodged to the side, something had crashed into his hip. And he remembers how Tillie had started the race running right beside him.

Geeger gasps.

And even though he won the race, the robot doesn't feel good at all.

One More Game

"TILL-*EEE*!" Geeger cries.

He rushes over to where she's still down on the ground.

By the time he reaches her, Tillie has let go of her knee.

She looks around, slightly **dazed**,

like she's not sure how she got there. Then she gives her head a shake and slowly climbs to her feet.

Geeger reaches out to help her.

"I—I—I—" he stammers. "I—are youuu—"

"I'm okay," Tillie says.

"I—I am SORR-eee," Geeger tells her. "I—"

Suddenly, Coach Keller is there.

"Are you all right, Tillie?" she asks.

Tillie nods.

And then Coach Keller turns to

Geeger. She smiles, reaches into her pocket—and pulls out the gold medal.

"This is yours, Geeger," she says. "Congratulations!"

Geeger takes the medal. But this moment—the moment he's been thinking about, dreaming about, hoping for, for days and days and days—doesn't feel anything like he thought it would feel. He's not happy. He's not proud.

"Geeger!"

It's Gabe, running up to Geeger and Tillie along with a bunch of their classmates.

"You won!" says Gabe.

"Congratulations!" Sidney says.

"You're even faster than the fifth graders!" adds **Mac**.

Geeger looks at Gabe, and realizes he doesn't know if his friend beat his Hula-Hooping record. He didn't even watch him. He totally forgot.

And Roxy—how did she do on the long jump?

And how was the kickball game?

Geeger really wishes he'd joined in on the kickball game. . . .

Suddenly, Geeger is **aware** of just how much he missed out on. Field Day is almost over, and he has been so focused on the foot-race and winning the gold medal, he forgot to have fun. And he didn't even eat a single bite of the special lunch Chef Mike cooked for him!

Worst of all, Geeger nearly hurt his best friend.

He looks at Tillie, then back at Gabe.

"Gabe?" the bot asks. "DID you *beeeat* your REC-ord?"

Gabe raises one of his eyebrows.

"By twelve whole minutes," he says.

Geeger grins, and then holds his gold medal out to Gabe.

"Huh?" Gabe says, staring at it.

"I would LIKE *youuu* to have THIS," Geeger says, shoving the big, shiny disk into his friend's hands. "Con-GRAT-u-LA-tions."

And before Gabe can say a thing, Geeger turns to Coach Keller. He whispers something to her, too low for any of his friends to hear.

"Well," Coach Keller says, "I suppose we do have some time left. . . ."

Then, nice and loud so the whole entire school can hear:

"ONE MORE GAME OF KICK-BALL! WHO WANTS TO PLAY? MEET ME ON THE FIELD IN FIVE MINUTES!"

Tons of kids dart over to the field.

But Geeger and Tillie hang back for a second.

Geeger asks, "Do you WANT to *plaaay*?"

Tillie grins and says, "Duh!"

And then, together, the friends race off toward the field.

Word List

assortment (uh•SORT•ment):
A collection of different things

attempts (uh•TEMPTS): Tries

aware (uh•WARE): The state of
knowing about something

bundles (BUHN•dulls): Groups of
a number of items that are packed
together

chanting (CHANT•ing): Reciting
words over and over again

clipboard (KLIP•bord): A flat

rectangular piece of material that holds papers with a spring device at the top

combinations (com•bih•NAY•shuns): Mixtures of different things blended together

competition (com•puh•TI•shun): A game or contest

daydream (DAY•dreem): To imagine something while awake

dazed (DAYZD): Stunned or shocked

disk (DISK): A thin, flat, round object

doubt (DOWT): A feeling of not knowing for sure

expanse (ek•SPANTS): A wide open area

expired: (ek•SPY•erd): No longer good to eat

hummingbird (HUM•ming•berd): A tiny bird with rapidly beating wings

memorized (MEH•mor•eyezd): Learned completely; committed to memory

participate (par•TIH•suh•payt): Join in an activity

preserve (pree•SERV): Keep safe from loss

springs (SPRINGS): Moves quickly

stash (STASH): Hide or store away

tempted (TEMP•ted): Made to want to do something

transformed (tranz•FORMED): Changed

Questions

1. Why does Geeger think he will be good at the footrace? What has he done to prepare for it?

2. Does your school have a Field Day? If so, do you have a favorite Field Day activity?

3. In this story, Geeger has several daydreams. Do you ever daydream? What sorts of things do you daydream about?

4. Geeger is so focused on winning the footrace, he almost forgets

to have any fun. Have you ever been so focused on doing one thing, you forget about everything else—even things that are very important?

5. What happens during the footrace? Who wins? Does Geeger feel how he thought he would feel at the end of it? Do you think Geeger is a good friend? Why or why not?

6. In Chapter 8, Geeger celebrates Gabe's achievement. Have you ever celebrated one of your

friends, just because? What kinds of things are your friends really good at? What do you think your friends would say YOU are really good at?